ISBN 978-1423157946
50599

EAN

The GUMAZING GUM GIRL!

CHEWS YOUR DESTINY

RHODE MONTIJO

Disney • HYPERION

LOS ANGELES   NEW YORK

Text and Illustrations copyright © 2013 by Rhode Montijo

First Hardcover Edition, August 2013
First Paperback Edition, June 2017
10 9 8 7 6 5 4 3 2 1
FAC-020093-17118
Printed in the United States of America

This book is set in 14-pt. Grilled Cheese BTN Condensed / Fontbros.com;
Grilled Cheese BTN Regular / Fontbros.com; Motter Corpus Std, Helvetica LT Pro / Monotype
Designed by Tanya Ross Hughes

Library of Congress Control Number for Hardcover: 2012036706
ISBN 978-1-4231-5794-6
Visit www.DisneyBooks.com

SUSTAINABLE FORESTRY INITIATIVE   Certified Sourcing
www.sfiprogram.org
SFI-00993

THIS LABEL APPLIES TO TEXT STOCK

For the mighty Kevin Lewis!

CONTENTS

CHAPTER I

A STICKY SITUATION

Gabby Gomez should have seen it coming.

She had been blowing on that bubble for as long as anyone could remember, and it was bound to blow up in her face sooner or later. But how could Gabby have imagined that something as sweet and as simple as one tiny piece of bubble gum could lead to such terrible trouble? Even with her parents and teachers always warning that no good would come from so much gum chewing and bubble blowing, it would have been hard to believe.

But then again, Gabby was far from your normal, average, everyday gum chewer. She chewed bubble gum everywhere.

She chewed it here.

7

She chewed it here.

She even chewed it here.

She chewed gum all day,
every day . . .

and all night, every night.

. . . Gabby woke up to a rather sticky situation.

She had gone to bed chomping on a huge wad of gum, and now it was stuck in her hair.

"*¡Ai, no!*" groaned Gabby as she waited for her mother to come to her rescue. "I'm never going to hear the end of this."

"There, there, *mi corazón*," cooed Mrs. Gomez. "This will take care of that sticky mess."

After witnessing her daughter's predicament, Gabby's mom had rushed out and returned with, of all things, peanut butter.

"Ewwww! Peanut butter?" asked Gabby.

Gabby Gomez did not like peanut butter.

"Yes, peanut butter," answered her mom. "Or I get a pair of scissors and cut it out."

"NO! That no-good Natalie Gooch would never let me live it down! I'd be the joke of the school." Gabby squirmed as her mom smeared the nutty goop into her hair.

"Hold still," soothed Mrs. Gomez. "Your *nana* used to swear by peanut butter for getting out gum . . . see?"

Gabby's grandma really knew her stuff about gum—or about peanut butter—because just like that, the gum was gone from Gabby's hair.

"Wow!" she exclaimed. "It really worked!"

And no lecture, either! Gabby thought. She congratulated herself on her narrow escape and rushed to get ready for school. "Now, let me wash off this yucky peanut-butter smell. . . ."

Gabby was peanut-butter-free
and dressed in no time flat.
"*Gracias*, Mami," she called as
she started out the door.
"*Adiós*. You too, Rico!"
But Mrs. Gomez had
something to say. . . .

"Not so fast, young lady."

Gabby's heart sank.

¡Ai, no! Here it comes, she thought. *Another lecture about chewing gum. Well, at least it's not from Papi. Nothing's worse than getting a gum lecture from a dentist.*

She had to act fast.

"But, Mami." Gabby smiled her sweetest and most innocent smile. "I'm going to be late. And you know how Ms. Smoot hates tardiness. Maybe this can wait until after school?"

And by then, hopefully, you will have forgotten this whole thing, she added to herself.

"Oh, this won't take long," replied Mrs. Gomez. "You'll have more than enough time to get to school."

Gabby's heart sank lower.

"Your father and I have warned you to go easy with chewing gum, haven't we?"

"Yes, Mami."

"Like the time at the art gallery. What a mess!"

"Yes, Mami."

"And don't forget about your *tía* Carmen's parrot. Poor Crackers! He never said another word. Your aunt never got over it!"

"I know, Mami."

"So, I'm sorry to have to do this, but . . ."

CHAPTER 2

A STICKIER SITUATION

"No more gum?! This is terrible! This is horrible!" Gabby dragged herself along the sidewalk to school.

After so many close calls, her mother had finally laid down the law. Now Gabby had no idea what she would do. The longest she had ever gone without bubble gum was the time that mean old Natalie Gooch had snatched her gum at the start of school. Gabby had been forced to go the whole day without a single chew, and that had felt like forever.

"This is the worst day of my life!" Gabby grumbled. She couldn't imagine it getting any worse. Not even if mean old Natalie Gooch sat on her.

Then Gabby remembered something. She reached down into her pocket and pulled out a piece of gum.

It was her very last piece of limited-edition
MIGHTY-MEGA ULTRA-STRETCHY SUPER-DUPER
EXTENDA-BUBBLE BUBBLE GUM.

The shiny sweet shone in her hand like a
rare gem. It was so pretty and pink, and
felt so smooth, and smelled so totally
scrumptious that Gabby could almost
taste it.

"Oh! It looks SOOOOOOO good. . . ."
Gabby licked her lips. "And just
imagine the bubble I could blow
with this!"

Gabby stopped herself.

"How can I even be thinking what
I'm thinking? Mami would have a
heart attack if she knew!"

But looking around, Gabby saw that there wasn't anyone to see her. . . .

Besides, she told herself, *it's just one teeny, tiny little piece. What could it hurt?*

And then . . .

"Oh, yum!" The flavors of the special, limited-edition MIGHTY-MEGA ULTRA-STRETCHY SUPER-DUPER EXTENDA-BUBBLE BUBBLE GUM exploded on Gabby's taste buds.

"It's so . . ." *Nom. Nom. Nom.* ". . . scrumptious!"

With every chew, Gabby's fears faded.

"It's so . . ." *NOM! NOM! NOM!* ". . . yummy."

NOM! NOM! NOM!

"And so . . ." *NOM! NOM! NOM!* ". . . gummy!"

All the awful things that had happened that morning—the gum in her hair, the peanut butter, even the lecture from her mother—began to feel like a bad dream. Soon any thought of getting busted had vanished. She wished the feeling could last forever.

"I bet . . ."

Nom! Nom! Nom!

". . . I could blow . . ."

Nom! Nom! Nom!

". . . the biggest . . ."

Nom! Nom! Nom!

". . . bubble . . ."

Nom! Nom!

". . . ever!"

Gabby took a long breath
and started to blow . . .

30

and blow . . .

31

¡Aí, no! Gabby thought. *What have I done?!*

Gabby stared at her hands in disbelief. They were a mess! But it didn't stop there. Gabby followed the sticky, chewy, gummy, gooey layer of pinkness all the way up her arms to her dress, then down her front to her legs and shoes. She was covered all over. She started to reach up to check her face and hair but knew she didn't need to. As anyone who has gone through a catastrophic bubble-gum bubble collapse knows, the face gets it first.

Gabby stood there completely buried beneath a coat of limited-edition MIGHTY-MEGA ULTRA-STRETCHY SUPER-DUPER EXTENDA-BUBBLE BUBBLE GUM. This was a bad situation.

Gabby was gummy.

I can't go to school like this, she thought. *Ms. Smoot doesn't even allow gum in class. But I can't go home, either. One look at me, and Mami would explode! She told me, "No more gum," and now I'm covered in it!*

DUN! DUN! DUN!

CHAPTER 3

STUCK!

Gabby wandered aimlessly, trying to figure out how such a small piece of gum could have created such a big mess.

"Look at me! This is crazy! *LOCO!*" she said in disbelief. "Mami said that all my gum chewing would lead to trouble, but did I stop? No! I couldn't stop chewing gum, and now I'm covered!"

It didn't make any sense.

"What was in that limited-edition MIGHTY-MEGA ULTRA-STRETCHY SUPER-DUPER EXTENDA-BUBBLE BUBBLE GUM anyway?" she asked herself.

But no answer could explain the amount of gum covering her. Or why it was impossible to get off. Anything Gabby touched stuck to her like she was made of glue.

"Aw, man!" she moped. "This stinks!"

It didn't take long for Gabby to realize the stuff covering her was not your standard, ordinary, candy-store-variety bubble gum. Far from it. This stuff was a whole lot stickier, and there was more of it than seemed possible. In fact, if Gabby hadn't known any better, she would have sworn that she was *made* out of gum.

"How did this happen?" Gabby wondered. "Why me?"

She felt low. She felt lower than low. Gabby felt as low as a wad of chewed-up gum scraped from the bottom of a shoe.

CHAPTER 4

A NUTTY IDEA

Suddenly Gabby Gomez didn't feel quite so low. How could she? Whatever had happened to her had given her some strange and wonderful new superpowers, and she had actually used those powers to help a stranger in need. She was like some kind of comic-book hero, swooping in to save the day.

Gabby grew so giddy imagining what else she might be able to do that she started to hum, and then to sing.

"If you start trouble, *doot, doot, doot*
I'll bust your bubble, *doot, doot, doot*
'Cause I'm a gum girl, *doot, doot, doot*
Yes, I am Gum Girl, *doot, doot, doot*"

She strolled along feeling quite pleased with herself until she remembered there was someplace she was supposed to be. "Oh, wait! I need to get to school. How do I turn back into myself again?!"

Gabby was stuck. *If only there were some magic potion that could make Gum Girl disappear and bring back my old self.* "Wait a minute. . . . Magic potion . . . Gum . . . Disappear . . ." Gabby jumped to her feet.

"Of course! That has to be it!" Could the answer
to her sticky bubble-gum problem be that obvious?
Gabby wasn't certain, but she wasn't going to
stand around waiting to find out. Having special
powers was neat, but when it came down to it, did
she really want to spend the rest of her life sticking
to everything?

Gabby set off like a bolt of lightning.

"This *has* to work!" she told herself. "Please, please, please let this work. If it does, I promise I'll never, ever sneak another piece of bubble gum as long as I live."

Gabby didn't even stop to wonder if she'd be able to keep the promise when she made it. She just . . .

. . . ran straight home.

Gabby was almost to the front door when a thought stopped her dead in her tracks. What if her mom still hadn't left to drop Rico off at preschool? Or had come back? Mami would freak!

I can't risk her seeing me like this, Gabby thought. *I'd never be able to explain.*

But a quick peek through the kitchen window put her fears to rest.

Nobody was home. She dashed inside, grabbed the jar of peanut butter, and ran to her room. It was time to test her theory.

"Ms. Gomez. So *nice* of you to join us."
Ms. Smoot stood in front of the classroom with
her arms crossed and a look that was anything
but nice. "Care to explain why you're late?"

Gabby felt like her mouth had been stuffed with
the stickiest bubble gum ever. She struggled for
an answer. "I woke up with gum in my hair," she
finally muttered.

"Unacceptable. Gabriella, I'm surprised at you.
You know I don't stand for tardiness. If this

happens again, you'll have detention. Now, please take your seat."

"Ha-ha! Look who got schooled," taunted Natalie Gooch.

Oh, great! thought Gabby as she sank into her chair. *Minutes ago I had superpowers. Now I'm being picked on by the biggest bully on the planet, and I'm powerless to do anything about it.*

CHAPTER 5

THERE AND BACK

"*Hola*, Mami!" Gabby rushed in after what had been her absolute worst day of school ever. Not only had she been chewed out by Ms. Smoot, but Natalie Gooch had spent the rest of the day teasing her for getting busted. "Uh . . . *adiós*, Mami!" She headed straight to her room. On top of everything else, she just couldn't face her mother.

"I'm making cookies for the bake sale at Rico's school," Mrs. Gomez called after her. "I think I'll make my famous peanut-butter cookies."

But Gabby had flown by so quickly that she didn't hear what her mother had said.

"Sounds great!" Gabby called back, and closed her bedroom door behind her.

She felt terrible. Why had she gone and broken Mom's no-gum rule? Then again, helping that lady get her purse back had made her feel there was nothing she couldn't do. Gabby had felt super. How great would it be to feel like that the next time mean old Natalie picked on her! But how?

Gabby stared hard at her hand, concentrating on turning into Gum Girl again. . . . But nothing happened.

Then she wondered if some sort of magic word might do it.

"Abracadabra," she commanded.

Still nothing.

"Juicy! Gooey! Soft and chewy!" Gabby chanted.

Nope.

She glanced over at her pillow. She always kept an
emergency piece of gum hidden under it, just in case
she needed some late-night chewing.

"What if . . ." Gabby pulled the gum from its hiding
place. Did she dare? What about her promise? What
if her mom walked in?

Gabby crossed her fingers and popped the gum
into mouth. She started chewing.

Nada.

This was her last chance. Gabby took a deep breath, blew a bubble, and waited.

Nothing. *Nada.* Nothing.

Feeling disgusted and defeated, Gabby let the bubble pop.

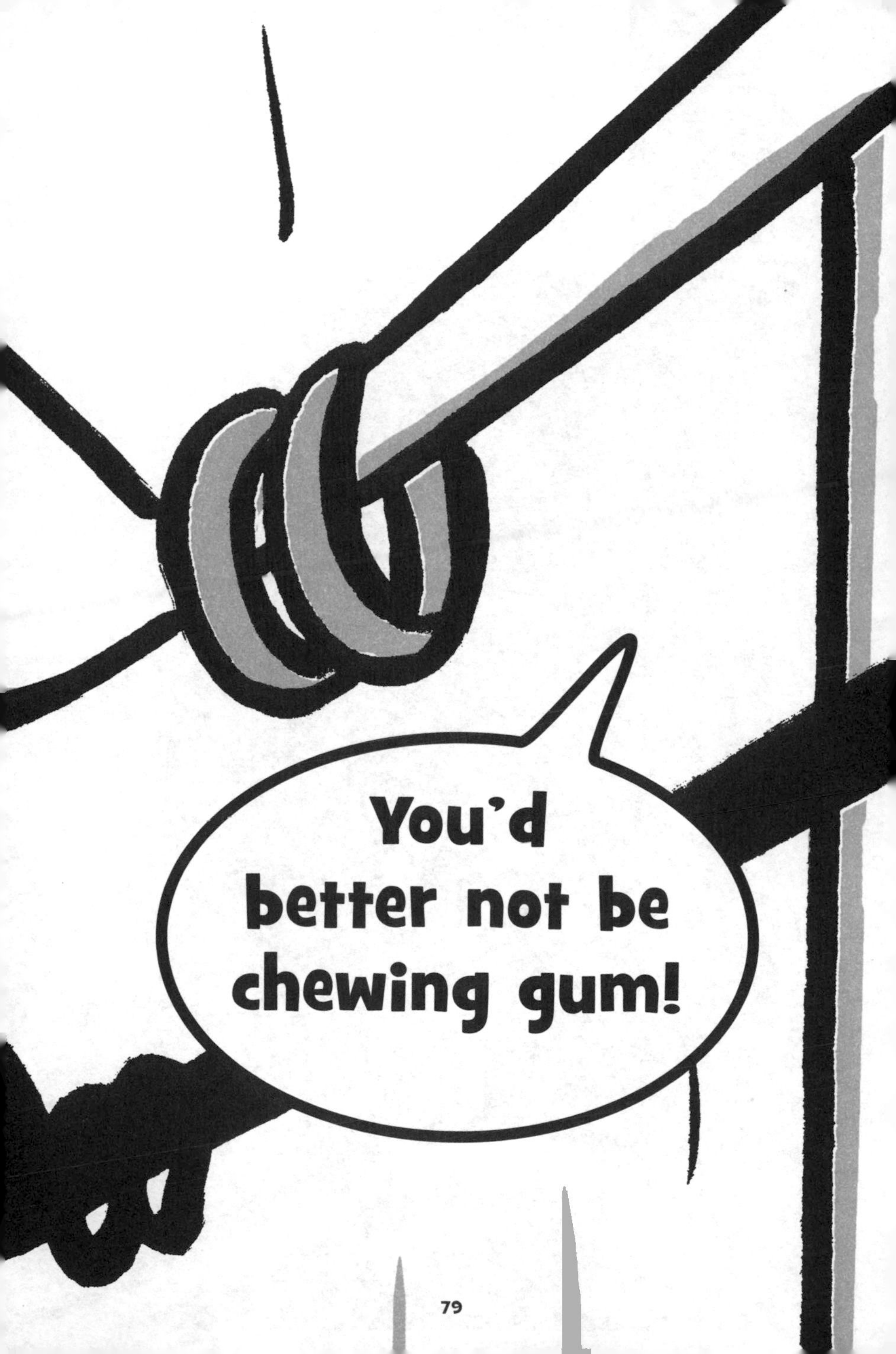
You'd better not be chewing gum!

"I thought . . . I heard . . ." Mrs. Gomez couldn't believe her eyes. "What are you eating?"

"Nothing. Just . . . uh, peanut butter," answered Gabby. "You know, this stuff's not so bad after all." She flashed her mother a wide peanut-butter grin.

"Here!" Mrs. Gomez reached for the jar. "Let me have that. I've been looking all over for it."

"It's all yours," replied Gabby. "I've had plenty. Yum!"

"Oka-a-a-a-y . . . then maybe you should . . . wash up. Dinner's almost ready."

CHAPTER 6

STRETCHED THIN

Over the next few days, Gabby got better and better at controlling her Gum Girl superpowers. She also got better and better at hiding them from her mom. In fact, she got so good at hiding her powers that she stopped worrying about her mom's rule against gum.

Besides, she asked herself, wasn't it good that she was helping people in need? Wasn't *that* more important than some silly rule against chewing bubble gum?

Every morning Gabby left for school with a piece of gum in her hand and a renewed sense of purpose in her heart. And every morning there were more and more people who needed her help along the way. And every morning Gabby tried to do it all. No task was too big . . .

or too small for Gum Girl.

Set . . .

Gabby got completely carried away with being a superhero.

First, she rescued a kitten . . .

. . . then she helped a little old lady cross the street. And after that . . .

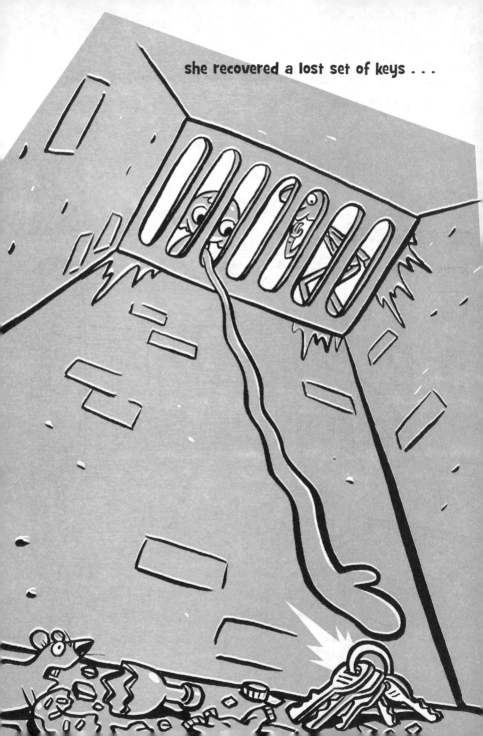

and stopped a runaway stroller.

Gabby was having a great time saving the day. But little did she know that her time was about to run out.

DUN! DUN! DUN!

CHAPTER 7

BUSTED

"Late again, Ms. Gomez?" asked Ms. Smoot the instant Gabby walked into the classroom.

Gabby had let time get away from her.

"I can explain," Gabby stammered. She had to think fast. What could she say that wouldn't give away her secret? "I . . . I . . . stopped to help someone . . . and lost track of time?"

"Really?" Ms. Smoot didn't budge. "Who? And *why* was that more important than getting to my class on time?"

Gabby just stood there, silent.

"I'm sorry, Gabriella, but you were warned. It's after-school detention for you." Ms. Smoot shook her head, disappointed. "And if it happens again, I'll have to speak to your mother. Now, take your seat."

Gabby couldn't let that happen, or else she'd be in serious trouble.

3

"Enough, Natalie Gooch!" Ms. Smoot shot to Gabby's defense. "I've also warned *you* about making fun of people. Well, young lady, since you think Gabby's punishment is so entertaining, you can keep her company. Detention for you too!"

Oh, great! It's bad enough that I've got detention . . . but now I have to spend it with Natalie? Gabby glanced over at her tormentor. Not only were her eyes glaring, but her nostrils were flaring too. The look was almost enough to make Gabby forget the trouble she was in for being late. Or the possibility of her mother finding out if she was late again. Almost.

Well, at least she can't just sit there staring at me for the rest of the day, Gabby thought with relief.

Gabby was glad when detention finally ended. She had to get home and get home fast! If her mom found out that she had gotten detention, there would be a million questions.

Right away, Gabby realized that her best bet was to turn into Gum Girl. Gabby Gomez could never make it home in time, but Gum Girl could make it there in no time. It would be close, but all she would have to do was change back before anyone saw her.

"This will be a **SNAP!**" Gabby grinned at the brilliance of her plan.

FILLMORE SCHOOL

Gabby hadn't
even made it close to home
when her perfect plan hit a
huge snag.

"Oh, snap!" cried Gum
Girl. "That plane is in
trouble!"

Forgetting everything
else, she sprang into action.
There was no time to waste.
Something had to be done,
and QUICK!

After the plane was safely on the ground, the entire airport erupted in celebration. The passengers and crew of Flight 808, as well as everyone in the terminal, cheered the brave little gum girl who had miraculously saved the day. Reporters from all over the city had witnessed the rescue from the ground and were descending upon the airport. Even the mayor showed up. Everyone wanted to know Gum Girl's story!

Gabby felt exhilarated.

"I can't believe I did it!" she whispered to herself "I can't believe I actually did it!"

She barely had time to think before questions began to fly at her from all directions.

"When did you realize the plane was in trouble?" fired a reporter.

"I was on my way home from school, and—" Gabby started.

A second reporter interrupted. "How did you figure out what to do?"

"Well, I—"

A third reporter broke in. "Where did you learn to stretch like that?"

Gabby's head reeled. As she tried to come up with something to say, one last, very young reporter broke through the noise with one last question.

Well, truth be told, it was more of a statement.

"You mentioned school," recalled this fourth reporter. "How old are you, anyway? Your parents must be proud to have such a brave and dependable daughter."

His question stuck in Gabby's brain. Even though she was doing good deeds, between the secrets she'd been keeping and the rules she'd been breaking, her life was turning into a sticky mess. And the guilt was becoming harder and harder to swallow.

All at once, Gabby felt neither brave nor dependable. She felt just the opposite—like a big, fat coward who her parents shouldn't even trust.

"Uhhh," Gum Girl stammered. "I think . . . I have to . . . get back . . . uh . . . to my secret . . . hideout. Yeah! That's right. My secret hideout."

And before anyone could ask another question, Gum Girl stretched her arm toward home.

Oh, man! she thought. *I should feel really great after saving all those people. But I just feel—* Gabby struggled for the word—*awful.*

Her mom and dad would be so proud of what she had just done. She knew they'd be. *But I can't even share it with them because I haven't been telling the truth.*

"That settles it," Gabby finally said to herself. "I have to admit what I did. I have to tell the truth. I just have to!"